Princess Poppy
The Hidden Jewels

Check out Princess Poppy's website
to find out all about the other
books in the series
www.princesspoppy.com

Princess Poppy
The Hidden Jewels

written by Janey Louise Jones
Illustrated by Samantha Chaffey

YOUNG CORGI

THE HIDDEN JEWELS

A YOUNG CORGI BOOK 978 0 552 56657 5

Published in Great Britain by Young Corgi,
an imprint of Random House Children's Publishers UK
A Random House Group Company

This edition published 2009

The Random House Group Limited supports The Forest Stewardship
Council (FSC®), the leading international forest certification organisation.
Our books carrying the FSC label are printed on FSC® certified paper. FSC is
the only forest certification scheme endorsed by the leading environmental
organisations, including Greenpeace. Our paper procurement policy can be
found at www.randomhouse.co.uk/environment

MIX
Paper from
responsible sources
FSC® C016897

Young Corgi Books are published by Random House Children's Publishers UK,
61–63 Uxbridge Road, London W5 5SA

www.princesspoppy.com
www.**randomhousechildrens**.co.uk

Addresses for companies within The Random House Group Limited
can be found at: www.randomhouse.co.uk/offices.htm

THE RANDOM HOUSE GROUP Limited Reg. No. 954009

A CIP catalogue record for this book is available from the British Library.

Printed and bound by CPI Group (UK) Ltd, Croydon, CR0 4YY

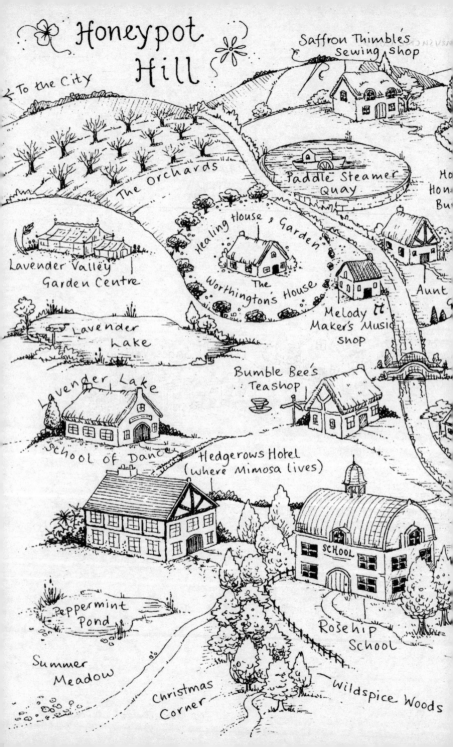

The Hidden Jewels
featuring

Princess Poppy

Honey

Daniel Bumble

Jasmine Bumble

Granny Bumble

Lavender Cotton
(Mum)

James Cotton
(Dad)

Arthur

Miss Mallow

Lilly Ann Peach

Chapter One

Honey flew down Poppy's front path like
a graceful fairy and ran into Honeysuckle
Cottage.

"Poppy!" she called breathlessly. "Where
are you? I've got some amazing news!"

Poppy appeared from her bedroom,
where she had been making a necklace.
"Hi, Honey! What is it?" she asked.

"Well," began Honey, "my mum and dad
are coming next week and they're going to
stay for a whole month."

Poppy was delighted for her best friend.

"Wow, Honey. That's so cool. I can't wait either. Your mum and dad are the best fun!"

Honey beamed from ear to ear. "I'm going to write the date on my calendar and tick off the days," she declared. "I can hardly wait!"

Honey spent the next week preparing everything for her parents' arrival. Together with Granny Bumble she spring-cleaned the cottage from top to bottom. Granny Bumble did lots of baking and even had her hair specially set by Lily Ann Peach at the Beehive Beauty Salon. Then the two of them got the spare bedroom ready, making up the bed with crisp white sheets and a cosy patchwork quilt. As a

finishing touch they picked
some pretty flowers in the
garden, arranged them in
a vase and put them on the
dressing table. Honey's mum
absolutely adored flowers.

After what seemed like an age the big day
finally arrived. The night before her parents
were due, Honey was in such a state of
excitement that she hardly slept a wink.
But now that the day had come at long
last, nothing else mattered. Honey simply
couldn't wait to see them. Every time she
heard a car drive through the village she
dashed outside in the hope that it was them,
even though she knew they weren't due until
the afternoon. At last, while Granny Bumble
was preparing tea, Honey heard another
car. This time she was sure it was her mum
and dad.

"Look, Granny, it's them!" she squealed as
she dashed out of the front door, down the

garden path and through the gate so that she could greet her parents at the roadside.

Honey fell into her mother's arms.

"Honey, darling, you look wonderful! And you've grown so much – you'll be as tall as me soon," gasped her mum.

"I've missed you, Mum," she said.

Before she really knew what was happening, Honey found herself being scooped up in a huge bear hug by her dad. Then he twirled her in the air until she was dizzy – just like he always did.

"And how's my fairy princess?" he asked. "Pretty as ever, I see."

Just then Granny Bumble came out of the cottage, smoothing down her apron, pushing an unruly curl behind her ear and smiling broadly. She was absolutely thrilled to see her son and daughter-in-law, and although she hadn't admitted it to Honey, she'd been so excited she hadn't slept a wink the night before either!

"Welcome! How are you? You must be exhausted after your flight. Come in and have some tea and then we can unpack the car," she said.

The Bumble family spent a relaxed evening together, catching up on everything they'd been doing since they last saw each other. Before long it was as if Honey's mum and dad had never been away.

The next day after school, Honey's parents, Daniel and Jasmine, were waiting for Honey and Poppy outside Rosehip School in their fancy hire car.

"Hi, girls! We're going on a mystery tour!" explained Daniel. "Poppy, I've spoken to your mum and she says it's OK for you come too!"

"Yippee!" cried Honey as she and Poppy climbed into the back seat.

As soon as their seat belts were fastened, the car sped off out of Honeypot Hill.

Daniel took lots of back lanes so that
Honey and Poppy had no idea where they
would end up. After a while they saw the
sea ahead, and the girls realized they were
driving towards Camomile Cove. Daniel
parked the car near the harbour and they
all got out and decided to have a wander
around the town. Poppy and Honey were
delighted to have a chance to show off
their favourite shops, Ned's Saddlers and
Bijou. They were even more delighted when
Honey's mum bought each of them a pretty
new handbag.

"And now for another surprise!" said Honey's dad as he led them back towards the harbour. "I've booked a boat ride across the bay."

"Yippee!" chorused Poppy and Honey.

"Can we have ice-cream sundaes in the Lighthouse Café afterwards?" asked Honey.

"Of course you can, sweetheart," smiled Jasmine, thrilled that their first outing was proving to be such a success.

For the first few days of the Bumbles' visit it was like one big holiday, even though it was still term time. Poppy and Honey were having so much fun. They went to a huge toy store in the city, dined in lots of lovely restaurants, played tennis and rounders, and had lots of get-togethers with other friends in the village. But after a week of fun Honey's dad began to feel rather restless. He was used to his phone ringing constantly and rushing from one meeting to another.

He simply wasn't good at not working.

One night, after her mum had put her to bed, Honey was thinking what a wonderful time she was having with her parents and imagining all the fun they would have together during the rest of their stay. She was feeling utterly content – until she overheard her parents talking in their room, which was right next to hers. Suddenly her happy little bubble burst.

Chapter Two

Daniel Bumble was complaining to his wife about life in the country.

"I think a month is going to be a bit too long in this village. I do love it here but I miss the buzz of LA and of always being busy. It's only been a week and I'm already bored," he complained. "It would be so good if Mum and Honey could come and live with us. I hate being apart from our little girl for so many weeks of the year. It would work out a lot better for us, Jas. We could have a normal family life. And I can't believe how hard Mum is working still. She acts like she's half her age. She deserves to take it easy now," he continued.

Honey held her breath, waiting to see what her mum would say.

"Daniel, we are *not* cutting this holiday short. I love it here – it's so beautiful and quiet and relaxing – and the best bit is that we get to spend all this time with Honey. I wish we could spend *more* time here, not less. You know that if she came to LA you'd hardly see her – you're always in the office, or away on location. That's why we decided it would be best for Honey to stay here with Granny, remember? You just need to get used to the slower pace of life and you'll love it here as much as I do. Imagine how Honey would feel if we left early."

Honey covered her ears with her pillow after that and tried desperately to get to sleep. She was really upset to find that her dad wasn't enjoying himself as much as she was. She was also worried about the idea of moving away. There was no way Honey wanted to leave all her friends and live in a new city in a different country. Thank goodness her mum seemed to be against the idea.

The next morning Dad was his usual chirpy self at breakfast and was dressed to go jogging. Because he was so perky, Honey wondered whether the conversation she had overheard had just been a dream. But in her heart of hearts she knew it hadn't been and she was determined to fix things.

"Hey, Honey, how about after school, you and Poppy take us on a cycle tour round the village. Would you do that?" asked her dad.

"OK, Dad, that sounds cool. We can take you to all our favourite places," said Honey, then ran all the way to school to tell Poppy what they were doing later.

Honey was distracted at school that day, worrying that her dad might go back to LA before the month was up or that he would make her move away from Honeypot Hill and all her friends. But this simply meant she was all the more determined to make the cycle tour really, really fun. She would show her dad how great life in the village was and that it definitely wasn't boring.

When the bell rang to announce the end of school, Poppy and Honey were the first out of the door. They had been thinking about the bike tour all day and couldn't wait to get started.

"This way!" called Honey as she cycled down the hill to Wildspice Woods.

The others followed her – Poppy on her smart red Warrior Princess bike, and

Jasmine and Daniel on the Cottons' bicycles.

"This is where we collect pine cones and twigs with Saffron for Christmas decorations," explained Honey breathlessly.

"Oh, I remember this place," said Daniel. "When I was a boy, we gathered conkers here every autumn and picked apples in the orchards in summer. If I remember rightly, we made a den in the trees here. It was kind of a secret base . . ."

Jasmine smiled as she saw Daniel relax a little, recalling his happy childhood in Honeypot Hill.

Then they made their way into Summer Meadow.

"I had such fun every Fair Day here, throwing wet sponges at the locals!" Daniel remembered.

"Did you like Fair Day, Dad?" asked Honey.

"Like it? I loved it!" he replied. "Especially the ice creams and fairground rides. And even the Fair Day Ball. You know, when I was out jogging earlier, I went through the grounds of Cornsilk Castle, where the ball always used to be held. I love that old place too."

"Dad, don't spoil the tour. That's exactly where we're going next!" said Honey.

"Great! I'll go by my secret route – race you!" cried Daniel.

Honey's mum rolled her eyes. "He's so competitive!"

"Yeah, and so are we!" Poppy grinned. "Come on. I know an even shorter cut!"

Poppy and Honey pedalled super fast, with Jasmine keeping up alongside them, and reached the grounds of the castle within minutes. But when they approached the castle itself, they saw, much to their annoyance, that Daniel was already there!

"Oh, Dan, you are a sly one – you'll have to tell the girls your secret route," said Jasmine with a smile, pleased that her husband was enjoying himself so much.

They all propped up their bikes and then spent a while just gazing at the impressive castle. Then they took a walk around the

17

grounds and Daniel read out what it said on the various plaques and information boards that were dotted about, most of which Poppy and Honey had never even noticed before.

"Come and look at this one, girls," he called. "It says here that the castle was built by the Mallière family. In fact I think I even did a project on it, way back when I was at the Rosehip School. The information on these plaques is definitely ringing bells."

Just then a tour guide appeared on the front steps of the castle and asked if he could help.

"Hi, Arthur!" said Poppy and Honey, who knew everyone who worked at the castle because they often played in the grounds.

"Hello, girls!" he replied.

"This is my mum and dad," said Honey proudly as she introduced her parents.

"Nice to meet you, Mr and Mrs Bumble," said Arthur.

"Likewise," replied Daniel. "In fact, you're just the man I'd like to talk to. I bet you know hundreds of stories about the castle. I remember a few from when I was at school but it's all pretty hazy."

"Well, I do know one or two." Arthur smiled at them. "Gather round and I'll tell you. The local archives say that the Mallières, the family who built the original castle, were accused of witchcraft hundreds of years ago. Despite their constant denials and the lack of proof, the rumours just wouldn't go away.

It is said that their lives were made so miserable by the gossip that they eventually fled the village so they could re-invent themselves elsewhere, poor souls. Another family took over the castle after that."

"Witchcraft!" gasped Poppy.

"Wow!" Honey shuddered. "Spooky!"

"The castle you see today was built in 1749, long after the Mallières had left," Arthur continued, "but they lived on this site for eight centuries before they were driven away."

"Ah, yes," said Daniel. "Now I'm beginning to remember. Wasn't there a medieval castle here first, with a drawbridge, moat and tower?"

"That's right!" enthused Arthur. "And that's not all! They say a beautiful princess was imprisoned here when her knight went off to war . . ."

Poppy and Honey *loved* the sound of that part of the story. They begged Arthur to tell them more but he had to hurry off home because his wife was expecting him for supper.

"Thank you, Arthur. That was fascinating," said Daniel, realizing that it was getting near their supper time too.

"Why not come back sometime soon for a proper tour?" suggested Arthur. "I'm around this Saturday if that suits you."

"That sounds perfect. We'd love to come back. Cheerio – see you on Saturday," replied Daniel.

Cornsilk
Castle
by
Daniel Bumble

Chapter Three

That night, after a delicious family supper,
Jasmine ran Honey a lovely deep bubble
bath. After that she tucked her into bed and
read her a story before kissing her goodnight
and turning out the lights.

"Mum, do you think Dad had fun today?"
asked Honey just as her mother was closing
the door.

"He had a brilliant day, pumpkin, and so
did I. Sleep well," said Jasmine.

Meanwhile Daniel and Granny Bumble
cleared away the supper things, chatting
away about the day's events as they did so.

"Do you remember that school project you did on Cornsilk Castle when you were about Honey's age?" asked Granny Bumble.

"Of course I do, Mum," he replied. "I got really into it."

"You certainly did!" she laughed. "You talked about nothing else for weeks – in fact, you're a bit like that now. I've never thrown any of your school things out, you know. That old project will be in the attic – why don't I go and have a look for it?"

"That's a great idea, Mum, but you put your feet up. I'll go."

On Saturday morning the Bumbles went over to the Cottons' house for brunch.

"Are you enjoying your stay, Daniel?" asked Poppy's dad, James.

"Oh, it's great fun. I thought I might not have enough to do here, but now that I've got into the history of Cornsilk Castle I'm not worried about that at all," he replied.

"I love that place and all its secrets. I found my old school project on it last night. There are quite a few questions I failed to answer back then, but I'm determined to get to the bottom of them now."

"I'm sure I did that project too!" said Poppy's mum, Lavender. "I love the story of the missing jewels of the princess who was once imprisoned there. It's just so mysterious!"

Poppy's ears pricked up at the mention of jewels.

"Ah! The famous jewels!" said Grandpa. "They've always been referred to as Princess Alyssa's jewels. Apparently they're made from the rarest and most beautiful precious and semi-precious stones – topaz, rubies, sapphires, diamonds, emeralds, amethysts, jaspers, moonstones and the like. They must be worth a fortune – if they really exist, that is."

"Well, I'm determined not only to prove

that they exist; with the help of Honey, Poppy and Arthur, I am going to find them!" said Daniel.

"Yippee!" chorused the girls.

Poppy, with her love of jewellery, princesses and mysteries, could think of nothing more wonderful than finding the gorgeous-sounding gems and discovering more about Alyssa, the medieval princess.

"Wow, it would be so amazing if you guys found the jewels," agreed Poppy's cousin, Saffron. "I can just imagine the princess and her maidservants in those elegant medieval gowns. I love that look so much! Maybe I'll design some medieval-inspired dresses in my next collection."

"Ooh, will you make me and Honey one?" asked Poppy.

"I'll see what I can do," smiled Saffron.

"Wow! Thanks, Saffron," said Honey, already imagining herself wearing a gorgeous medieval gown.

"I can't wait until Monday," Poppy said excitedly. "I'm going to tell Miss Mallow all about this at Circle Time. She loves history, doesn't she, Honey?"

Honey nodded. She was excited about Princess Alyssa's jewels too, but mostly she was just happy that her dad seemed to be enjoying himself. Her cycle tour of the village had worked!

As soon as the scrumptious meal – free-range eggs, local sausages, grilled mushrooms and golden toast, all washed down with freshly squeezed orange juice and breakfast-blend tea – was over, Daniel looked at his watch and stood up.

"Thank you, Lavender and James, that was a most delicious meal – I shan't need to eat again for days! I'm afraid that the girls

and I have got to go now. Arthur offered
to give us a full tour of the castle today
and we need to pop into the library on the
way," he explained.

"It's a pleasure," replied Lavender. "Good
luck with the detective work."

"Thank you!" said Daniel. "Girls, are you
ready?"

"I just need to get my bag," replied Poppy.
"I'll meet you in the hall."

She ran to her room
and put a notebook
and torch in her bag.
Cousin Daisy had
taught her to always
be prepared during
any sort of investigation.

Ten minutes later Poppy, Honey and
Daniel arrived at the library, which was in
the Village Hall. Daniel led the girls straight
to the history section and soon found what
he was looking for. He took two books from

the shelf: one about medieval history and one called *Honeypot Hill Through the Ages*. Just then, Honey spotted another book.

"Dad, look at this one," she said. "It's all about medieval English. Should we borrow this too?"

"Well done, darling!" replied Daniel. "I'm sure that will come in handy. Now let's check these books out and get to the castle!"

When they arrived at Cornsilk Castle, they found Arthur pacing up and down in the hallway wearing his guide's uniform.

"Hello!" he beamed. "I'm ready for the tour if you are."

"We certainly are," replied Daniel. "The girls haven't been able to talk about anything but the castle, the jewels and the princess since our last visit."

"Um, that's all *you*'ve been talking about too, Dad!" laughed Honey.

"Well, since you've all been eagerly

anticipating it, let's get started!" said the
old guide, glad to have such an interested
audience. "We'll start at the bottom and
work our way up. Follow me to the vaults
– these were part of the castle that was here
from 1100 AD. Health and Safety say we all
have to wear hard hats down there, so here
you go," he continued, dishing out bright
yellow hats to everyone.

They set off on their tour, with Poppy
and Honey feeling nervous and excited all
at the same time.

"Are you sure we won't be imprisoned,
just like the princess?" Poppy asked.

"And it won't be too dark down there,
will it?" asked Honey.

"I promise we'll be all right," said Arthur.
"I have keys for every door here and we'll
be able to see just fine. There are lights and
I've got my torch."

"Me too!" said Poppy.

They went along a maze of corridors,

then through a doorway that seemed to separate the newer part of the castle from the original. All of a sudden they were in what remained of the medieval castle.

"Wow!" gasped Poppy. "This is amazing!"

Chapter Four

"This was the chapel of St Stephen in
the first fortress," explained Arthur as they
looked around the beautiful old room with
a painting of St Stephen above the altar.
"It's the only remaining structure from the
original medieval castle – besides the vaults,
of course. We believe this is where Princess
Alyssa would have worshipped every day.
Even though the legend says she was held
captive, she was apparently still allowed to
pray. We don't normally show it on tours
as it wouldn't stand up to a lot of traffic, but
once in a while we bend the rules if visitors

are really enthusiastic. Below this are the vaults, and under the altar is the Knights' Vault, where they say some famous knights were laid to rest."

Poppy and Honey couldn't believe what they were seeing and hearing. They'd had no idea that there was a lovely old chapel right in the heart of the castle.

Arthur led them behind the altar, where there was a wooden trapdoor in the floor. He lifted it up to reveal a wooden staircase like a ship's ladder, which led down into the vaults within the deep, dark foundations of the castle.

"What exactly *are* the vaults, Arthur?" asked Poppy, peering down the stairwell.

"They're a labyrinth of

cellar-like rooms, dating from the 1100s," he explained. "There are definitely some tombs down there. I suppose they might also have been used to hide family secrets from the outside world."

"Do you think the jewels might be down there, Arthur?" asked Honey.

"It's certainly one of the places they could be," he replied.

"Wow!" said Poppy. "That would be so cool!"

The whole tour party climbed carefully down the wooden ladder.

"It's said that the spirit

of a knight haunts the vaults," explained
Arthur as they all made their way down,
"but I've never seen anything."

Just as he said this, Poppy shone her torch
into the blackness to reveal a suit of armour.

"Aaargh!" screamed Honey, grabbing her
dad's hand. "It's the ghost of a knight. Look!"

"Don't worry, Honey, it's just a suit of
armour," Poppy reassured her best friend.
"I think it's really cool."

"It certainly is," agreed Daniel. "I wonder
what else we're going to find."

"I'd forgotten that was down here," chuckled Arthur. "I remember it gave me quite a fright the first time I saw it too. I was convinced it was moving towards me!"

"Arthur, do you think Alyssa was a *real* princess?" asked Honey, changing the subject.

"I'm sure she was," replied Arthur. "But because everything we know about her and her jewels has been passed down by word of mouth, most people think it is just a myth. If we could find some real evidence, then we could prove all the doubters wrong."

They walked silently along the dark, damp corridors. The vaults lined the main passages. Some had metal-barred doors, which made them look like prison cells.

"I expect these were cells originally," observed Daniel.

"Yes, indeed they were — but as for Princess Alyssa, legend has it she was kept in a circular room at the top of a tower. Unfortunately this tower was demolished when the newer castle was built. But from what I've read about the building in the archives, the tower was close to the chapel, so if she did exist, I think Alyssa was imprisoned directly above where we are now," explained Arthur.

Poppy shuddered. She simply could not imagine how it must have felt to be trapped in a small room, day after day. Poor Princess Alyssa!

As they continued along the torch-lit corridor, Poppy tripped over a pile of rubble. When she recovered her balance, she looked down at the ground and shone her torch there.

"This part of the floor looks like it has been lifted or dug up or something," she said.

"Come and have a look."

The others made their way over to where Poppy stood. Arthur began to move the rubble aside with his hands. A plume of dust rose into the air, making Poppy and Honey cough and splutter.

"Is there anything under there, Arthur?" asked Daniel.

"Well, I'll be blowed! I think there is. Can you give me a hand with shifting this debris? I think I can feel something underneath it," he replied.

They all got down on their hands and knees in order to clear away the rubble.

"Nearly there – we just need to shift a few more stones and we'll be able to see what's here," said Arthur.

Within minutes he had freed an ancient-looking book. The writing inside it was just like the writing in the book on medieval English they had borrowed from the library earlier that day.

Arthur shone his torch on it to get a better look. Then Honey's dad took the library book out of his bag and started flicking through it, trying to match up the old-fashioned words and letters with modern ones.

"I think it says *Lucky Charms and Tinctures, by Princess Alyssa of Avalon*."

Honey gasped. Poppy's eyes opened wide. "Wow!" she said. "If this was written by the princess, then it's proof that she was real!"

"You're right," said Arthur. "It certainly looks like the princess was more than a figment of local imaginations down the centuries, doesn't it?"

"Um, Dad, what are tinctures?" asked Honey.

"They're a bit like potions," explained Daniel.

The girls pondered on this for a moment.

"Does that mean she really *was* a witch?" asked Honey.

"It doesn't prove it, but it does tell us that there might be some truth to the stories," replied Daniel. "I'd like to study this book, with your permission, Arthur, and come back for another look round when we know a bit more about the princess and her potions."

Arthur nodded. "Good idea. You're welcome to borrow it, as long as it comes back in the condition we found it in. I think we've all had enough excitement for one day. Good work, everyone!

Now that they had made one good find, Poppy and Honey were more determined than ever to solve the mystery of Princess Alyssa and the hidden jewels.

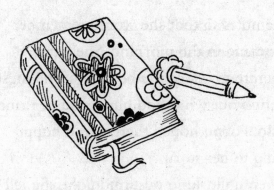

Chapter Five

That night, as she fell into bed, exhausted, Poppy imagined that she was the princess waiting in the locked castle, not knowing when she would be released.

That poor princess! she thought as she wondered how old the princess was when she was imprisoned, what she looked like, where she came from, how she got to be a princess in the first place, and what her lucky charms and tinctures were.

With all these things racing around in her mind Poppy just couldn't get to sleep. She decided to turn on her light and jot down some notes so that she would remember everything in the morning. She was desperate to get to the bottom of the mystery and find out what had happened to Princess Alyssa. Poppy hoped there was a happy ending to her story.

Eventually, long past midnight, she fell asleep, her mind still whirring with thoughts of knights, princesses, castles, jewels and witches.

The next morning, straight after breakfast, Poppy dashed over to Honeypot Cottage to see if Honey's dad had worked out what was in the charm book. She arrived to find Honey and her father both poring over the book, with Daniel making notes.

"Hi, Poppy!" they both chimed.

"Any ideas about the charms yet?" she asked.

"Well, the book of medieval English we borrowed from the library is really useful.

Honey and I have been translating the charms but it's taking a while," explained Daniel. "Why don't you come and help us?"

Poppy settled down at the table and took out her notebook. She began to copy out some of the charms and then cross-reference them with the library book, almost as if she was doing a puzzle.

"Here's what I've got so far," said Poppy after about fifteen minutes.

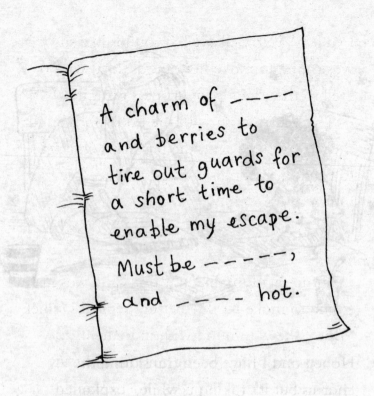

A charm of _ _ _ _
and berries to
tire out guards for
a short time to
enable my escape.
Must be _ _ _ _ _,
and _ _ _ _ hot.

"I think it says 'boiling hot' at the end there," said Daniel.

"That fits," agreed Poppy. "But what are the other missing words?"

"I know!" Honey exclaimed suddenly. "I think it says 'herbs and berries' and then 'brewed'!"

"That makes sense, well done!" agreed

Daniel. "Well, well, well. It sounds like she was trying to make her guards dozy with a spell so that she could escape. Poor girl!"

They carried on with the book and found that it was filled with the princess's charms to bring her knight back or heal her heart or make time go faster.

"I don't think Princess Alyssa was a bad witch, was she?" concluded Poppy.

"It doesn't look like it. I think she was just trying to make her life better," replied Daniel. "But if she was found with ingredients for charms, then they might have thought she was a witch – in those days they thought all witches were bad."

"I noticed something else in the book," said Poppy, carefully picking it up and turning to the back. "Look at this," she continued. "It could be some sort of secret code."

"Wow, that's so cool!" exclaimed Honey. "I wonder what it means . . ."

On Monday morning during Circle Time at school Poppy told the rest of the class all about the mystery of the hidden jewels and the imprisoned princess. Everyone was absolutely fascinated, especially Miss Mallow.

"Do *you* think she was a witch, Miss Mallow?" asked Poppy.

"It doesn't sound like she was, from what you have said. At least, not like the evil witches on broomsticks we imagine," Miss Mallow replied. "Poor, poor Princess Alyssa. How awful to have been locked up like that."

"Me and Honey are going find out the truth about her!" exclaimed Poppy. "And with the help of Honey's dad and Arthur we're even hoping to find her jewels too!"

"Well, we all look forward to hearing how you get on," said Miss Mallow. "Good luck!"

After school, Honey's dad took the girls for a snack at Bumble Bee's Teashop. Honey's mum was down at the Beehive Beauty Salon having some treatments done.

"Three strawberry milkshakes, please, Mum. And three of your best cakes too!" said Daniel.

"Coming right up!" smiled Granny Bumble, choosing three iced cakes.

Daniel carefully carried the milkshakes and cakes over to the table where Poppy and Honey were sitting. The girls were chatting non stop and poring over Poppy's notebook.

"What are you two plotting?" asked Daniel as he sat down.

"Nothing, Mr Bumble. Me and Honey were just writing down the things we *do* know about Princess Alyssa – and some questions about the things we don't know yet," explained Poppy.

"Great!" he replied. "Can I see?"

Poppy nodded and passed him the notebook.

Princess Alyssa:

What we know so far by Poppy Cotton and Honey Bumble.

① She was locked in the tower part of the old castle.
WHY?

② She made spells to help her get out and they thought she was a witch.

③ Did she escape?

④ Her jewels have been hidden in the castle.
WHERE?

⑤ She had a secret code in her charm book. What does it mean and can we crack it?

⑥ The Mallières who owned the castle vanished without a trace. Where did they go and what happened to them?

"Wow! I'm impressed, girls," said Daniel. "You are asking all the right questions. I think we need to go back to the castle next Saturday and carry on looking for some answers."

"Yippee!" chorused the girls. The weekend could not come soon enough.

On Saturday morning, on her way to the kitchen to make breakfast for everyone, Granny Bumble noticed an envelope lying in the hall.

"It's too early for the post," she muttered as she picked it up. She saw that it was addressed to her son and that it had been delivered by hand.

She laid the table and propped up the letter by Daniel's place, then set about making porridge.

Honey was the first one down and spotted the envelope right away. "Dad, there's a letter for you," she called. "Come

down and open it – I want to know who
it's from!"

"Morning to you too," said Daniel as he
came into the kitchen rubbing his sleepy
eyes. "You are a nosy parker, Honey. It's not
even addressed to you! Mum, did this arrive
this morning?"

"Yes, dear, it was lying in the hall when
I came down," replied Granny Bumble.
"Whoever delivered it is certainly an
early bird."

"Come on then, open it. What if it's a
letter from an admirer – I've got a right to
know!" laughed Honey's mum.

Daniel opened the envelope and read the letter, looking more and more confused as he did so.

"Well, what does it say, Dad?" asked Honey.

All eyes were on Daniel.

"Um, I think it's a sort of riddle. Listen:

Princess Alyssa:

She wasn't a witch, she was good and true,
Please help to show her as she is due.
Help you will find, if you follow this clue:
What I can tell you is known by few.

Go to the Keep Tower, down by the lake,
Stand by the oak, and to east five steps take.
Turn to the left, and look to the ground.
If you dig for it, the clue you have found.

What you find here is a missing piece:
Find where it fits, but do not cease.
Wherever it fits, you will find
Clues and words of every kind.

"Who on earth could have sent that?"
asked Granny Bumble.

"I don't know, but it's someone who's
trying to help you guys solve the mystery,"
said Jasmine.

"Or send us off in the wrong direction, perhaps?" suggested Daniel.

"People round these parts don't act that way," said Granny Bumble. "I think it's genuine help all right – but from whom? That's what I'd like to know."

The letter was printed from a computer so there was no handwriting to give them any idea who wrote it.

"I think the first thing to do is check out this clue – we can work out who sent the letter afterwards," said Daniel. "Honey, phone Poppy and tell her to be ready in half an hour – and her dad too, if he's around. I'll ring Arthur and let him know that we'll be there at ten – oh, and that he should bring spades, tools and a wheelbarrow! That will have him guessing!"

Chapter Six

Poppy and her dad were very excited when Honey told them about the new clue, and they were over at Honeypot Cottage in a flash. Poppy simply could not believe this exciting and romantic story had happened right here in her own village. She was used to playing in the courtyard, visiting her friend Sweetpea, who lived in a cottage in the grounds, and going to lots of local events and parties at the castle. The story and the new clue made shivers run down her spine – she was desperate to find out the truth.

"What I want to know," announced Poppy,

"is whether or not the knight returned and if Princess Alyssa lived happily ever after. Oh, and where the jewels are hidden, of course!"

"Me too," said Honey.

The girls wore jeans and wellies as they knew that digging in the grounds was likely to be a mucky job. They walked through the village, following their dads, who were deep in conversation about the riddle. Before long they arrived at the fountain in front of the castle, where Arthur was waiting for them. He was ready with spades and a wheelbarrow and was keen to hear all about the mysterious clue.

"Well, it says here that we must go to the Keep Tower by the lake and look for an oak tree," explained Daniel. "But where is the Keep Tower?"

"We know!" cried Poppy, before Arthur could explain. "Don't we, Honey?"

"Yes, follow us!"

The girls had often played near the tower

and knew the area around it well, so they
led the group down to the edge of the small
lake behind the castle, where the old keep
tower stood.

"This is the tree here," said Arthur, pointing to a vast old oak. "What next?"

"It says here that we must take five steps to the east and then turn to the left," said Daniel, re-reading the riddle and following the instructions.

They each grabbed a spade – Arthur had kindly found a couple of smaller ones for the girls. Five steps to the east of the tree, Daniel marked out a circle with some big stones.

They started to dig. It was hard work and Poppy was turning over nothing but earth. It seemed as if they were getting nowhere. Daniel was starting to think that someone *was* playing a mean trick on them.

"Perhaps there is someone with a pair of binoculars over there in the woods, laughing away at us right now," he whispered to James.

"Let's carry on for ten more minutes," said Poppy's dad. "It would be a shame to give up now."

Just then Poppy's spade hit something hard. She didn't like to say anything immediately in case it was only a stone, so she dug a little deeper. She had definitely found something – she began to smooth away the earth to see what it was.

"I think I've got something here," she told the others.

Everyone came close. Daniel and Arthur dug a little more around the edges of Poppy's find. They tried to lift the object out of the ground. It was a solid stone block with something engraved on it, but because it was so filthy they couldn't make anything out clearly.

"Let's put it in the wheelbarrow and take it up to the castle courtyard," suggested Arthur. "We can wash it with the hose there and see what it says."

Poppy was thrilled that she had found the clue. She and Honey couldn't wait to find out what secrets it revealed.

Chapter Seven

Poppy and Honey hosed down the stone tablet. The words on it were in medieval English, so Daniel got out his library book. Before long they had managed to decipher the letters and found a message.

The princess is a bird in a cage: her knight
with sword and shield doth forge into battle.
But she awaits him like a delicate rose
that will not wither with time.

"Now, Daniel, tell us the rest of the riddle," said Arthur.

Daniel reached into his pocket. "It says, *What you find here is a missing piece. Find where it fits, but do not cease.*"

"Right, so this tablet must fit into a pattern of similar stones," concluded Arthur. "Now, I'm sure I've seen stones like this in the castle somewhere."

He scratched his head for a long time, picturing every room in the castle, and then seemed to be struck by inspiration. "Follow me and bring the tablet with you! Oh, and you'll need the hard hats. We're going into the old castle again."

Arthur led them into the ancient chapel once more. When they reached the altar, they all looked up at the painting of St Stephen. But Arthur pointed down to his feet. "No! Look below!" he said.

They saw that the ground beneath them was made up of stone tablets. All had engravings on them except one, which was totally plain.

"Aha!" said Daniel. "Our tablet must have been moved from here and replaced with this plain one. There must be something hidden under it. Let's lift it out. Maybe the Mallières set up this quest."

"Do you have a tool we could lever the tablet up with, Arthur?" asked Poppy's dad.

"Yes, I'll be back in a minute," said Arthur, who couldn't quite believe what was happening in the usually sleepy castle.

Poppy and Honey were very impatient to see what was under the floor.

"What do you think we'll find?" asked Honey. "I hope it's not something spooky!"

"I think it will be Princess Alyssa's jewels!" Poppy replied, with her fingers crossed.

When Arthur returned a few moments later, he and Daniel carefully levered up the tablet. It came away surprisingly easily.

"It's not heavy stone!" said Arthur. "It's much lighter – how strange. This must have been someone's hidey-hole."

Daniel nodded. "I'm not sure why they hid the real one under the tree though. It seems like a lot of effort. Maybe whoever did this planned to replace it one day."

Once the tablet was up, they shone the torch down into the gap and saw a vault beneath them.

"Can we get down there?" asked James.

"We have to. I'm certainly not stopping now," said Daniel as he tried to lower himself through the space. He almost got wedged in the narrow gap. "Too many of Mum's delicious cakes, I'm afraid!" he joked. "I'm never going to squeeze through."

"I'll go!" offered Poppy. "I'll fit through."

It was true that her small body would slide more easily through the space left by the tablet, but none of them liked the idea

of sending Poppy into a deep, dark vault
– especially since they didn't know what
was down there.

"What would Mum say?" said Dad as
Poppy begged him to let her go.

"We don't have to tell her," suggested
Poppy.

"Poppy, you know we don't keep secrets
in our family!"

"Please, Dad, we have to find out what's
down there," said Poppy.

Her dad thought through the situation again and curiosity soon got the better of him. "Well, the only way I'll let you go down is if we tie a rope around your waist so that you can let us know whenever you want to come back up," he said.

"Sounds like good idea," said Daniel, but Honey looked concerned.

"I'm staying out of it," said Arthur. "I know what her grandpa, my friend Joseph Mellow, would say if he was here!"

Honey thought Poppy was being incredibly brave – she could think of nothing worse than being pushed down a small hole into the dark, creepy vaults of a medieval castle, but her friend was far too excited to feel afraid.

Poppy got rigged up with a rope and was given instructions on how to pull on it if she wanted to come back up or needed more slack.

"Poppy, if you need to be lifted up, tug

three times," said her dad. "If you need to
walk on further, pull once, sharply. Do you
understand? And of course you can shout
up to us too."

"OK, Dad. I just hope I find something
cool," she said, imagining the wonderful
jewellery glinting in the dark.

"Good luck!" said Honey.

Poppy had butterflies
of excitement and
anticipation in her
tummy as she was
lowered into the dark
space. As she descended
on the rope, she shone
her torch into the vault
below. It was filled with
elaborate tombs, all
inscribed with dates and
messages, and smelled of
murky old water, which
lay in puddles on the

uneven floor. As soon as her feet touched the
ground she began to regret her bravery and
longed to be lifted straight back up to the
chapel, but she knew the others were relying
on her – and she was absolutely determined
to find something connected with the princess.

Poppy's eyes soon got used to the gloom
and she began to take in her surroundings in
detail. There were swords and shields as well
as rubble and old bottles. After a while she
spotted a wooden box lying in one corner

70

of the vault. She tugged for more slack on
the rope and went over to have look.

"I've found a box," she called out.

"Bring it up then," replied her dad. "Let
us know when you're ready to be pulled
up, darling."

Poppy picked up the box, walked back
across the vault and pulled three times on
the rope. She was sure she had found what
they wanted. Soon Poppy and the box were
being lifted out.

"Well done, Poppy!" said Arthur. "What a brave girl!"

Her dad hugged her. "I can't believe I let you do that. You are brilliant!"

Poppy felt very relieved to be back with the others again. Now that it was over, she could hardly believe she'd done it either!

"Well, come on then! Let's see what's inside," said Daniel.

They lifted the lid and the first thing they saw was a magnificent jewel-encrusted cross.

"Look," said Arthur as he examined it, "there's an engraving on the back. It says, *To AA from GL, 1456*."

"How fascinating!" said Daniel, delighted that the riddle had turned out to be a real clue.

"AA has to be Alyssa of Avalon but I wonder what GL stands for. Do you think these are the famous jewels?"

"I don't think so," replied Arthur. "The village stories speak of tiaras and necklaces – a whole treasure trove. I think this is another clue to the real treasure."

Underneath the cross were some faded yellow papers tied together with a deep purple ribbon. Arthur carefully took them out of the box.

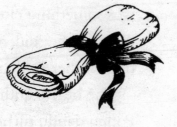

"They're letters. I think they're letters from Alyssa to her knight while he was away at war," he said. "This is quite a find – well done, everyone."

"Does that mean he definitely came back to her then?" asked Poppy hopefully. "Otherwise, how could her letters to him be here?"

"I'd like to say that was the case, but

someone else could have brought the letters
back here. But let's hope you're right, Poppy!
I'm a sucker for a fairytale ending too!"
said Daniel. "I'll have a proper look at them
later – I'm sure they'll shed some more light
on this."

Poppy had another peek in the box – there
was something else there, right at the bottom.
"Look!" she said, reaching inside. "There's a
tiny leather Bible in the bottom of this box!"

The others gathered around her again.
Poppy gently turned the pages over and
found that there was some writing in the
back of the Bible.

Alyssa of Avalon, the Chapel of St. Stephen, pew three, seat two

"Maybe that was where she sat in the chapel," suggested Arthur. "Let's have a look."

They all went over to the pews to try to work out exactly where the princess had sat to worship and gain comfort while her knight was away. Honey went to the third pew back, found the second seat along and started looking around. Before long she had discovered a drawer under-neath the seat.

"There's a message in here!" she called as she pulled something out of the hidden drawer.

"Do you need any help reading it?" asked Daniel.

"Thanks, Dad, but it's in normal English – a bit like the riddle you got this morning," replied Honey, and then read out what it said.

You have succeeded where
others have failed.
You have followed the clues,
And as you are committed,
You deserve to find the jewels
The gems are not where they
seem to be —
The magic number to count
is three.
Pillars made from golden blocks
Conceal a very beautiful box.
Inside that box, you will
honestly find
Sparkling gems of every kind.

"You were right, Arthur, the jewels *are* somewhere else," said Daniel. "Come on, we must go straight into the main castle and look for the golden pillars!"

Poppy was exhausted but dashed along behind the others with Honey, unwilling to give up now. She wanted to be there when they found the jewels!

Chapter Eight

They all stood in the main entrance of the castle and studied the new riddle.

Arthur scratched his head. "But there just aren't any golden pillars as far as I know," he said.

"Perhaps there used to be?" suggested Daniel.

"I suppose there could have been. Let's go to the Archive Room, where we keep sketches and paintings of the castle over the centuries. Maybe that will shed some light on this," suggested Arthur, who was also dying to work out the riddle and find the legendary jewels.

They followed him into the Archive Room. It was quiet and dark and had cream cotton blinds drawn down over every window.

"Everything is listed in date order. See – here we have artefacts dating from the seventeenth century, here we have the eighteenth, and so on," explained Arthur.

"Why don't we each take a century and check through the images of the castle from that period?" suggested Daniel.

Everyone agreed: they put on white cotton gloves to protect the old documents and began searching through hundreds of drawings and documents. It seemed as if this would be a fruitless task, when all of a sudden Honey, who was looking through the nineteenth-century pictures, found something.

"Come and see this!" she called out, brandishing a small picture dated 1865. "Golden pillars!"

The others stopped what they were doing and raced over as though their lives depended on it.

"She's right! Do you recognize the pillars in the picture, Arthur?" asked Honey's dad.

Arthur smiled. "Yes, I do. Follow me!"

In a matter of minutes they were back at the front entrance of the castle. When they looked around, they could see three black pillars.

"Oh!" exclaimed Poppy. "Did these used to be gold?"

"Yes, they must have been – clever girl!" replied Arthur. "These are certainly the pillars shown in the picture. The jewels must be hidden around here somewhere – unless this is yet another clue."

They examined the pillars but could find no secret cubby-holes or any other possible hiding place – until Poppy suddenly glanced down.

"Look!" she said. "There's a hatch in the

floor here at the bottom of this pillar." She
tried to open it but had no luck.

"I'll go and get my tool kit from the
chapel," said Arthur.

"What does the riddle say again, Dad?"
asked Honey.

"It says, *Pillars made from golden blocks conceal
a very beautiful box . . .*"

"Oooh, this really could be it this time!" squealed Honey.

Arthur returned and used his claw hammer to open the door, then shone his torch into the hole. The girls held their breath.

"It looks like a safe. It's got a fancy dial on the front," he said.

The girls jumped up and down with excitement. If the jewels were inside, it would make the whole story complete.

"The only problem," said Arthur, pulling on the safe door unsuccessfully, "is how to crack the code so that we can open it."

Daniel tried to pull open the door from every angle, then Poppy's dad had a go at twisting and turning the dial.

"It's no use," he said. "We're never going to get this open without the code."

"This is so annoying!" said Poppy. "We've got to crack the code! Let me have a closer look."

"I suggest we call it a day now," said

Arthur. "We're tired out and not thinking straight. We might have some fresh ideas tomorrow."

Poppy and Honey were terribly disappointed to be going home without solving the mystery and seeing the jewels, but their dads agreed that they needed some time to think everything through. They went their separate ways, all feeling very frustrated that the last piece of the puzzle was still baffling them.

That night Poppy couldn't sleep. She was determined to solve the mystery and find the jewels so she switched on her bedside light and took out her notebook.

It wasn't until she got to the last page that a flash of inspiration came to her. On this page was the code she had copied from the back of the charm book they had found the week before. The caged bird, the crown, the sword and shield and the rose matched the symbols on the dial of the safe. She'd cracked the code!

Poppy ran downstairs to tell her dad.

"Look!" she cried. "These symbols are in a certain order. Maybe if we line up the symbols on the dial of the safe into this order, it will open the door! We must go and see – I can't wait until the morning!"

"Poppy, I like your idea and you may be on to something, but it's late, darling, and Arthur is the only one with the keys."

"Pleeease, Dad! It's really important. I won't sleep a wink until I know what's in that safe," begged Poppy.

"Well, I'll phone round and see what everyone says," agreed Dad.

When he'd finished talking on the phone, he told her, "We're meeting at the castle at six a.m.

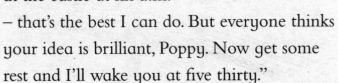

– that's the best I can do. But everyone thinks your idea is brilliant, Poppy. Now get some rest and I'll wake you at five thirty."

Poppy reluctantly returned to bed, and when her dad shook her awake in the early hours, she was up in a flash.

Chapter Nine

They met the others at the castle entrance just as the sun was rising, and Poppy led the way to the safe. She worked on the combination on the dial, based on the code of the bird, the sword and shield, and the rose. Within minutes, the door fell open to reveal a gold-edged card.

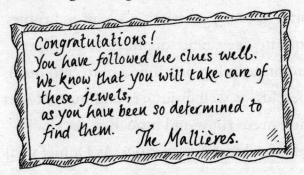

Congratulations!
You have followed the clues well.
We know that you will take care of
these jewels,
as you have been so determined to
find them.   The Mallières.

"We've found them!" Poppy exclaimed. "The card says so, look!"

Arthur gently pulled a decorated wooden chest out of the safe. It was covered with intricate golden patterns and jewels. "You open it, girls," he said.

Poppy and Honey took one side of the box each and lifted the lid.

"Wow!" they gasped as they were dazzled by an array of glittering jewels.

"Gosh!" said Arthur. "How beautiful – they're even more impressive than all the local stories said they were!"

Poppy and Honey were both silent with wonder as they feasted their eyes on the precious jewels. There were sparkling stones of every description – vast red rubies, exquisite deep-blue sapphires, clear white diamonds, milky pearls and glittering green emeralds, as well as jaspers and moonstones. There were rings and brooches, necklaces and bracelets, even earrings. As Daniel very

gently rummaged in the box, he came across
a fabulous tiara, encrusted with diamonds,
pearls and deep red rubies.

"Princess Alyssa's crown!" said Poppy. "Wow! These jewels are amazing. I can't wait to tell everyone about this in Circle Time tomorrow. Miss Mallow will definitely want to see these. She makes lovely jewellery but it's not quite like this!"

"I think all the local folk will definitely want to see this treasure," Arthur agreed.

"I reckon there will be queues all round Honeypot Hill to view these beauties!" said Poppy's dad.

"Well, fancy that!" said Arthur. "I've been walking past this treasure every day for the last thirty years. I can't believe it. I'd better get ready for a busy few weeks around here."

"Hey, girls, there's something at the bottom of the box," said Daniel.

He slid a piece of paper carefully out of the box, unfolded it and began to read what it said to the rest of the group, referring to the medieval English book when he needed help.

April 1455

A poem for dear Alyssa

Dearest Alyssa, my own fairy bride
While I am gone, I pray thee will hide.
Sit in the tower with the lock
turned fast,
And that way, my dear, our true
love will last.

I will return on my mighty white
steed
If these instructions ye will fast
heed.
With local folks do not mingle or mix,
Count the months I am gone,
not more than six.

Then you will see me cantering by
Past the river and forest alongside the
rye.
I will look on your face, perfect and
true.
Remember, Alyssa, I will always
love you.

"It's signed 'Sir Gawain Laverok'. It must be a poem from the knight to the princess," he said.

Poppy and Honey could hardly believe what they had found. The knight had wanted Princess Alyssa to lock herself away until his safe return because he loved her so very much and was worried for her safety.

"But *did* he come back to her?" asked Honey, unable to bear the suspense.

"Of course he did, Honey! Isn't it wonderful!" said Poppy.

"What do you mean?" asked Daniel. "How can you be sure he returned?"

"Well, the poem was written in 1455 by Gawain Laverok – 'GL' – when he must have left her. But the jewelled cross from the box was given to her by 'GL' in 1456 – one year later! So he came back! Of course he did. I just knew it!"

Chapter Ten

Arthur wrote down the code for the safe and placed the jewels back in there. "These will have to go to a museum eventually, but let's keep them safe here until all the local people have had a chance to see them," he said.

"Yes, let's throw a party for the villagers before we hand them over," agreed Daniel. "A medieval party!"

"Yippee!" said Poppy. "I hope Saffron will make us those medieval dresses, Honey!"

Honey smiled. "Me too! That would be brilliant."

"The only part of the mystery we still have

to solve is who sent me the clue which got us started on the quest," said Daniel. "It would be nice to thank that person."

"That might always be a mystery," said Poppy's dad as they headed for Bumble Bee's Teashop for a hearty breakfast.

The Medieval Knights and Princesses party was to be held one week later in the Great Hall at Cornsilk Castle. Lily Ann Peach's Beehive Beauty Salon was packed all week as all the ladies of Honeypot Hill wanted to look their best. Saffron's Sewing Shop had also been frantically busy as she had designed a medieval-inspired range in honour of the discovery of the jewels.

"We're so lucky that we were actually there when they were found, aren't we, Saffron?" said Poppy as they tried on their princess gowns on Saturday morning.

"Yes, you are very lucky indeed. I'm so proud of you for solving the mystery

and for proving that the story of Princess
Alyssa and her knight was true after all!"
said Saffron. "I can't wait to see the jewels
– everyone in the whole village is dying to
see them – or that's what my customers have
been telling me anyway."

Granny Bumble had organized a
wonderful spread of food and drinks using
medieval recipes that she had discovered in
the Archive Room, and Arthur had agreed
to dress up as a medieval court jester to
entertain the guests.

When it was time to get ready for the party,
Poppy was both nervous and excited. She
slipped into her deep-red medieval princess
dress, and as she looked in her long mirror, she
felt a link to Princess Alyssa. She finished her
outfit with a tiara encrusted with red sparkly
stones and went to collect Honey.

Poppy and Honey had been given the
job of greeting all the guests as they arrived
at the castle.

The girls were thrilled by the efforts everyone had made. All their friends arrived, looking wonderfully glamorous in medieval-style gowns, with great hairstyles and pretty, sparkling headbands. Miss Mallow, who was especially interested to see the jewels as she loved local history and also designed jewellery in her spare time, arrived wearing a gorgeous white chiffon medieval fairy dress. Poppy and Honey decided that if there had been a competition for the best outfit, then Miss Mallow would definitely have won it – she looked amazing. The last person to arrive was Lily Ann Peach. Poppy didn't like to say so, but she didn't look her usual stylish self. Her hair was a terrible sight.

"I didn't have time to do my own hair!" she laughed, patting her messy mop. "But I'm not missing this, not for anything!"

The jewels were beautifully presented in a velvet-lined cabinet with spotlights shining on them. Everyone gasped at their beauty. It was a very exciting moment for the villagers. During the speeches, Honey's dad explained how they had discovered the jewels and then read out a poem he had found among the papers they had retrieved from the vault. It had been written by the princess herself, but Daniel had translated it into modern English for the benefit of the audience.

"*My long months of lonely waiting are done,*
My knight has returned, I have borne him a son.
We are happy here living as husband and wife,
In a perfect world, with a perfect life.

My soldier protects me all that he might,
We can only live by the rules of the knight.
Of valour, of honour and a love so true,
These are the purest of rules, of real virtue."

Poppy and Honey smiled from ear to ear, and the local people fell in love with the princess just as they had.

"If the kind person who has helped us enormously by delivering the riddle is present, could he or she please come forward?" continued Daniel. "We want to thank you for enabling us to unravel the mystery and for helping us locate the exquisite jewels which are on display for the whole community to enjoy."

At first no one moved, but then there was a movement in the crowd. Poppy gasped with surprise when she turned to see who had stepped forward. It was her teacher, Miss Mallow! Poppy didn't understand. How could Miss Mallow have had the riddle, and why did she keep it a secret?

Miss Mallow took the microphone from Daniel Bumble. "It was me. I'm sorry to have been so secretive. When I was a teenager, my grandmother told me the riddle. She

explained that we are directly descended from Princess Alyssa and the knight, but that over the years the Mallière family – or Mallows, as we became two hundred years ago – denied the link. The reason for this was the hurtful accusations of witchcraft. These accusations began when it was discovered that Princess Alyssa had made potions to bring her knight back or to free her from the castle so that she could go to him. She missed him so much. It seems that she was treated cruelly and locked up by those her knight had left to care for her. We changed our name from Mallière to Mallow to leave behind rumours of witchcraft that made the lives of my ancestors such a misery in this village. The Mallières fled the village in the 1600s, when witchcraft was an obsession, but returned in the 1800s with the new name. It may have been at this time that one of my ancestors set up the quest for the jewels. The riddle is the only thing I had and I didn't

know where to begin. But I shall be for
ever grateful to Daniel, Poppy, Honey,
and of course Arthur, for solving the mystery
of the hidden jewels and telling the village
this lovely, romantic story!"

The crowd cheered. Holly smiled happily.
She was thrilled to have the proper story
told and to have such an interesting family
history.

"I am proud to be related to the princess
and I hope the whole village can enjoy the
story now."

"Wow, Miss
Mallow!"
said Poppy,
approaching her
teacher. "This is
the coolest thing
ever! My teacher
is related to a
real-life princess.
You are so lucky.

I wish I was – I would never keep such a cool thing a secret. So are the jewels yours?"

"I don't think so, Poppy," laughed Miss Mallow. "They will go on display in a museum but I will copy some of the designs for my new jewellery collection."

"From now on, you will always remind me of Princess Alyssa," said Poppy.

Her teacher hugged her. "But don't forget that you are a princess too – every little girl is!"

THE END

Read a chapter from
Princess Poppy's next adventure,

Happy Ever After . . .

Princess Poppy
Happy Ever After

Chapter One

Poppy was very excited. She had just received
an invitation to her first ever barn dance. It was
to be at Barley Farm the following Friday, and
the theme was country and western. She raced
over to see Honey right away to talk about
their outfits, and with a little help from Granny
Bumble they had soon both decided on red and
white gingham dresses and cowboy hats.

On the day of the dance Poppy dressed with
great care and turned to admire herself in her
bedroom mirror. She particularly loved the
fringed cowboy boots that Mum had found
in a charity shop, and her big Stetson hat.

"Yee-haa!" she said to herself as she did
another turn in front of the mirror.

"Come on, Poppy," called Mum. "You must
be ready by now! We're going to miss Farmer
Meadowsweet on the bucking bronco if we don't
go now!"

"Just coming, Mum," replied Poppy as she
grabbed her things and ran down to meet the
rest of her family.

"I'm going to try that bucking bronco too!" said Dad. "I bet I can stay on the longest!"

"Well, make sure you don't hurt yourself!" scolded Mum. "Right, let's go then."

Dad took Poppy's hand and they giggled together as they made their way down to Barley Farm with Mum walking beside them.

"Remember we can't be late home," she told them. "Grandpa can only babysit the twins until nine. And, James, don't drink too much punch – it's really potent, apparently."

"Yes, dear!" replied Dad, rolling his eyes and winking at Poppy.

Sometimes Mum was no fun at all.

When they arrived at the farm Poppy could hardly believe her eyes. Farmer and Mrs Meadowsweet had gone to so much effort – it looked just like a scene from one of the old cowboy films that Grandpa liked to watch. There was a huge tent set up next to the big barn, and colourful banners and bunting garlanded the farmyard. There were games and

near the tent, with tables set out all around it, laden with crisp salads, spicy sauces, crusty bread and fat herb sausages, and the air was filled with the most delicious cooking smells.

"Hi, cowgirls!" said Poppy as she ran to greet Honey, Sweetpea and Mimosa, who were all standing together near the entrance to the barn. "This is so cool! You all look amazing! Where's Abi?"

"Oh, she's got a violin exam tomorrow so her mum and dad said that she had to practise tonight," explained Sweetpea.

"Oh, shame, she would love this," said Poppy.

"Let's go and look at the bucking bronco," suggested Mimosa.

"Ooo, yeah, let's," said Honey.

"Come on, then," replied Poppy. "Follow me!"

The four friends made their way to the meadow, where the crazy rodeo-style "bull" was in action. Farmer Meadowsweet was holding on for dear life and looking very red in the face. Mum had been right – this was definitely too good to miss. He looked so funny. As they stood there watching, Cousin Saffron's husband, David, came over and told them that the farmer has been practising on it all week because he wanted to be able to stay on for two whole minutes.

Poor Farmer Meadowsweet looked as though his arms were about to fall off – this seemed like the longest two minutes ever.

there was no way she could have said anything to her father – she was laughing so much she couldn't get a single word out!

"Quick! Someone do something!" wailed Mrs Meadowsweet. "This is not good for a man of his age!"

But just then, the farmer let go of the bull and tumbled off onto the hay below in a crumpled heap.

"I told you I could do two minutes, didn't I?" he chuckled, exhausted. "Now, who's going to help an old man up?"

Sally's boyfriend, Sol, who was a doctor in Strawberry Corner, rushed over to help the farmer up and check that he was OK.

"I think he'll live, but he'll need a glass of punch to revive him!" Sol announced to the guests, and a big cheer went up.

"Now, he's the sort of doctor we need round here," said Farmer Meadowsweet merrily.

Poppy's dad was next up on the bucking bronco. He whispered to Poppy that he was going to better Farmer Meadowsweet's record by staying on for a full three minutes.

Poppy watched nervously as her dad clung onto the bull and was very proud indeed when he broke the record. He could hardly walk afterwards but luckily Mum didn't notice as she was busy throwing hoops onto a cone, trying to win teddies for the twins. Poppy knew what Mum would have said if she had seen Dad hobbling around: "Told you so!"

"Well, I think I deserve some of that punch now – don't tell your mother, Poppy!" Dad smiled. "I'll see you girls later."

Poppy, Honey, Mimosa and Sweetpea decided that it was time to try some line dancing so they headed over to the big barn. The steps were being called out by Len, the lead singer of The Cattlemen. All the villagers were having a wonderful time stepping to the beat, with calls of "Yee-haa!" every now and then! The girls joined in immediately and soon got the hang of it.

After a while Mum came over to say that it was time to go home, but just then Poppy

noticed Farmer Meadowsweet climbing up
onto the hay-bale stage and walking over to
the microphone.

"Please can we stay, Mum – just to hear
what he's going to say?" she begged.

"Someone's got to get back for the twins but
I suppose it doesn't need to be all of us.
I'll go and you and Dad can stay," agreed Mum.

"Thank you, Mum!"

Poppy and Dad kissed Mum goodbye and
turned back to look at the stage.

"It is wonderful to see so many of you here tonight," began the farmer. "This barn dance is just our way of saying thank you to everyone for buying local produce and keeping us in business! Well, that is one of the reasons for the party. The other reason – and the most important one, I think – is to share some very special news with you. My beautiful daughter Sally is getting married to Sol Melville. Mrs Meadowsweet and I cannot wait for him to officially be part of the family – the son we never had. I mean, Dr Sol *Meadowsweet* sounds good, doesn't it?" he joked.

There was a huge cheer and lots of laughing and shouts of "Congratulations!" and "About time too, Sal!"

Poppy was thrilled at the news – she simply adored weddings.